W9-BRX-784

Valparaiso Public Library
103 Jefferson Street
Valparaiso, IN 46383

WHO NEEDS IT?

PORTER COUNTY PUBLIC LIBRARY

Valparaiso Public Library
103 Jefferson Street
Valparaiso, IN 46383

vjjfi VAL
MAY

May, Eleanor
Who needs it?
33410013041001 10/29/14

by Eleanor May
illustrated by Blanche Sims

Kane Press, Inc.
New York

For the students and staff of Kipps Elementary—E.M.

To Kelly MacAskill and Billy and Henry Sims—Love, B.S.

Text copyright © 2009 by Eleanor May
Illustrations copyright © 2009 by Blanche Sims

All rights reserved. No part of this book may be reproduced or transmitted in any form or by any means, electronic or mechanical, including photocopying, recording, or by any information storage and retrieval system, without permission in writing from the publisher. For information regarding permission, write to Kane Press, Inc., 240 West 35th Street, Suite 302, New York, NY 10001-2506.

Library of Congress Cataloging-in-Publication Data

May, Eleanor.
Who needs it? / by Eleanor May ; illustrated by Blanche Sims.
p. cm. — (Social studies connects)
"Economics/Wants & Needs-Grades: 1/3."
Summary: When best friends Gus and Mickey go camping, Gus wants to put his survival skills to the test while Mickey brings everything from pizza to a television set.
ISBN 978-1-57565-281-8 (alk. paper)
[1. Camping—Fiction. 2. Survival—Fiction. 3. Best friends—Fiction. 4. Friendship—Fiction.] I. Sims, Blanche, ill. II. Title.
PZ7.M4513Who 2009
[E]—dc22

2008026609

10 9 8 7 6 5 4 3 2 1

First published in the United States of America in 2009 by Kane Press, Inc.
Printed in Hong Kong.

Book Design: Edward Miller

Social Studies Connects is a registered trademark of Kane Press, Inc.

www.kanepress.com

Mom said I can camp out in the woods behind my house tonight. It'll be just like my favorite book, *Alive and Well*!

I've read *Alive and Well* four times. It's about a lost kid who survives in the wilderness with nothing but what she has in her pockets—three paper clips, a stick of gum, and a plastic spork.

Okay, our woods are not exactly wilderness. But I'll take what I can get!

I call my best friend Mickey and ask him to camp out with me.

"I don't know, Gus," he says. "I've never been camping. What is there to do?"

"Lots of things," I tell him. "In *Alive and Well,* the girl traps a rabbit with her shoelace, discovers a stream full of gold nuggets, and weaves a blanket out of wild grass and bark. And that's just on the first day!"

ALL YOU NEED

A **need** is something we *must* have, something we can't do without. All human beings need food, water, clothing, and shelter (a safe place to live).

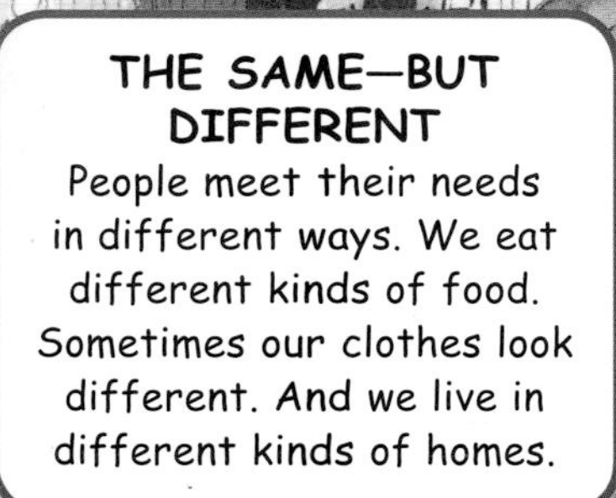

THE SAME—BUT DIFFERENT
People meet their needs in different ways. We eat different kinds of food. Sometimes our clothes look different. And we live in different kinds of homes.

I start to get ready. I don't have a spork, so I look for other things that are pocket-sized. My mini-flashlight. A granola bar.

My sister Sonia pokes her head into my room. "Heard you're camping out. Want to use my tent?"

"No, thanks!" I say. "We can always crawl into a cave."

The doorbell rings. It's Mickey.

"What is all that?" I ask him.

"My—" *huff, puff* "—air mattress," he wheezes. "And a few other things."

GOTTA HAVE IT?
A **want** is something we would *like* to have—but could do without. A new bike, a pretty necklace, a soccer ball. We all have different wants.

WANT OR NEED?
It can be hard to tell the difference between a want and a need. If you went camping what things would you want to take with you? What things would you need?

I stare at Mickey's gigantic pile of stuff. "We're going *camping,"* I say. "Roughing it. You're only supposed to bring what you really need."

Mickey looks surprised. "But I *did* bring only what I really need."

I roll my eyes. "Whatever."

We pack up and head out.

A few steps into the woods, Mickey flops down on his air mattress.

"Maybe I don't actually *need* this," he gasps. "I can pick it up on our way back."

IT'S YOUR CHOICE!

It sure would be fun if we could have everything we wanted! But what if we can't carry it all—or can't buy it all? Then we make choices. We get one thing and do without another.

I take a deep breath of woodsy air.

This is great! Here I am, surviving alone in the wilderness. Maybe I'll rescue a wolf cub that has lost its pack. It'll be my friend and follow me everywhere. Of course, there's also Mickey. . . .

Wait a minute. Where *is* Mickey?

Holy cow. Was all that stuff in his backpack?

"Who needs a beach chair in the woods?" I say.

Mickey grins. "I do, after hauling that huge pack around! Want some lemonade?"

I sigh. We don't *need* lemonade. Then again, I didn't bring any water. And I sure am thirsty.

"I'll have a little sip," I mumble.

I WILL SURVIVE!

Just try living without food and water. Actually—don't try it! We all need food and water to stay alive. People have survived for weeks without food—but only a few days without water.

After ten minutes of trying to stuff everything back in his pack, Mickey gives up.

"The thermos is empty, anyway," he says. "I'll pick it up on the way home."

Even without the lemonade, Mickey still lags behind. I wait for him on a log by the creek.

I spot something sparkling under the water. Could it be a gold nugget?

I can't quite reach it. Maybe if I stretch a little farther—*ZZZZZZOOOM!* Something whizzes by me. I lose my balance and—*SPLASH!*

Sputtering, I get to my feet. I open my fist and find a . . . bottle cap. So much for striking gold.

Mickey dashes up. "Oh, no! My monster truck! Since you're in the water, can you get it, Gus?"

The wet truck won't start, so he leaves it to dry.

I can't believe what Mickey thought he'd need. An air mattress? A beach chair? A toy truck? He must have brought everything in his closet.

The sun dries me quickly. I munch on my granola bar and feel better. After all, I'm a survivor!

I picture myself coming out of the woods. Reporters crowd around. *How did you do it, Gus?* they ask me. *Gus? Gus?*

"GUS!" Mickey is yelling. "Can't you hear me? Wait up!"

Hmm. That gives me an idea. "Hey, have you got any dry clothes in your pack?" I ask Mickey.

"Nope," he says cheerfully. "Good thing I don't need them, huh?"

I squish away without answering.

KEEP YOUR SHIRT ON!

We don't have tough skin like elephants, or fur like bears, or feathers like ducks! Clothes protect our bodies from both the blazing heat and the freezing cold.

Mickey limps toward me. “I’m getting a blister,” he moans. “Did you bring a Band-Aid?”

“Nope,” I say. “Good thing I don’t need one!”

Mickey flops to the ground. “I can’t take another step. Let’s camp here.”

“Okay,” I say.

Soon my stomach starts growling. I wish I'd brought more food.

In *Alive and Well,* the girl ate grasshoppers. . . .

Who knew they'd be so hard to catch?

When I trudge back into camp, Mickey waves. "You missed the best part of the movie, Gus."

I blink. "You brought a *TV*?"

"Yeah, but the picture's getting blurry." Then he grins. "Luckily I brought some DVDs, too."

THINK!

Most families have only a certain amount of time and money. They have to take care of their needs (like food) before their wants (like TVs). So when you want something, try asking yourself, "Do I really *need* it?" You might be surprised at your answer!

I show Mickey what I caught for dinner.

He stares at me. “Wouldn’t you rather have a slice of pizza?”

“Pizza is for wimps,” I say.

Okay. I open my mouth, close my eyes . . .

Hey! Where’d it go?

Oh, well. It didn't look too yummy, anyway.

Things could be a whole lot worse, I tell myself. Sure, I'm a little hungry. But at least I'm warm and dry.

Uh-oh. Was that a drop of rain?

"Quick!" I say. "Get out your umbrella."

Mickey's face turns pink. "Um . . . I don't have it. It was poking me, so I left it on the trail."

I look at his overstuffed backpack.

"You didn't happen to bring a tent, did you?"

"Nope," he says glumly. "You?"

I shake my head.

GIVE ME SHELTER!

A good shelter protects us from bad weather and helps keep us safe. The most important shelter of all is our own home.

In *Alive and Well,* the girl built a lean-to. It kept her cozy in a blizzard.

But we get soaked while we hunt for branches. And our lean-to leaks.

Mickey says, “Look, I don’t want to be a party pooper, but . . . could we go home?”

“YES!” I say. “I mean, if *you* really want to.”

We set off. It's lucky I brought a flashlight. Still, it's hard to see where we are going.

"Are we almost there? This pack is heavy," Mickey grumbles.

Up ahead, I see a clearing. . . .

Oh, no! Our lean-to! We've gone in a circle.
We're lost!

Mickey glares at me. "Why didn't you bring a compass so we could find our way?"

"Me? What about *you*?" I demand.

He shrugs. "I brought lots of other stuff."

"Yeah," I tell him. "Stuff we didn't need."

"Well, you hardly brought *anything* we need!"

I stomp on ahead. If that's the way he feels, Mickey can just find his own way in the dark.

Oomph!
I slip—on Mickey's beach umbrella.

Now I'm even madder. Why couldn't he have brought something useful, like those colored paper clips the girl used in *Alive and Well* to mark the trail when—

Wait a minute. Mark the trail?

I rush back to Mickey. "I found your beach umbrella!" I tell him. "That means we must be going the right way!"

We find Mickey's monster truck next,

and then his lemonade thermos.

Last of all, we find the air mattress. We're home!

We sit by the fire and toast our toes. I tell my mom how we got lost in the woods and found our way home.

She smiles. “Glad you’re both alive and well.”

“Next time,” I promise, “we’ll bring everything we need.”

“And *only* what we need,” Mickey adds.

He starts scribbling out a list: *Stuff We Need for Our Next Camping Trip.*

"Our *next* camping trip?" I ask. "You mean, you want to go again?"

"Of course!" Mickey says. "But I'm not sure I want to eat grasshoppers."

I laugh. "Then don't forget the pizza!"

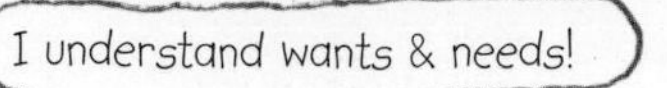

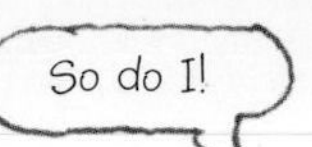

MAKING CONNECTIONS

What a campout! Mickey brings stuff that he *wants*, but much more than he really *needs*. Gus hardly brings anything!

There are some basic things we all need to survive: *food, water, clothing,* and *shelter.* So the next time you catch yourself thinking, "I really need that"—maybe you don't!

Look Back

- On page 6, Gus's sister offers to lend him something. Is it a want or a need? What answer would you have given her? Why?
- What does Mickey say on page 8? Do you think that's true?
- What does Gus need on page 15? How about on page 18?
- On page 23, how do Gus and Mickey try to take care of one of their needs? What happens?

Try This!

Pretend you're going on an overnight campout. Look at the pictures. Which things would you put in your backpack? (Remember—you have to carry everything you bring!) Explain why you made your choices.